Star Friends

HIDDEN CHARM

LINDA CHAPMAN

ILLUSTRATED BY LUCY FLEMING

stripes

IN THE STAR WORLD

The trees in the forest glittered with stardust. In a secret clearing, a wolf with silver-tipped fur gazed into a pool of mirror-like water. A picture on the surface of the pool showed four girls sitting in a circle, each with a young animal beside them. The wolf's gaze lingered longest on the girl with shoulder-length dark-blond hair. The fox cuddled up to her had large pricked ears, a white tip to his bushy tail and a cheeky look in his indigo eyes.

The silver wolf's ears twitched as a snowy

owl came flying through the black sky with a soft hoot. He landed on a tree branch beside her, his feathers shining. A stag with magnificent antlers stepped silently from the shadows and a badger came shuffling out of the bushes.

"Greetings," said the wolf.

The stag looked at the picture in the forest pool. "Are you watching our friends in Westcombe village again?"

The wolf nodded. She and the other elder Star Animals used the magic pool to watch over the young Star Animals who had travelled to the human world. Each animal had to find a child to be their Star Friend. They taught that child how to use the magic current that flowed between the Star World and the human world to do magic and help people.

"Maia and her friends have learned a lot about magic since they became Star Friends," said Hunter the owl.

"But they have not yet solved the latest

mystery," the badger said, watching as the red squirrel whisked up the arm of the girl he was sitting by and tickled her with his tiny paws. "They do not know who conjured the Shades that caused so much trouble last week."

Shades were evil spirits who lived in the shadows. They could be conjured by people using dark magic and trapped inside everyday objects. They brought chaos and misery wherever they went, and Star Friends had to work with their Star Animals to send them back to the shadows.

"It is an unusual case this time," said Hunter thoughtfully.

"It is, but anyone using dark magic must be stopped – whatever their reasons," said the stag.

"Let us see if the Star Friends in Westcombe can find out the identity of the person before more trouble comes," said the badger.

The animals nodded and settled down to watch.

CHAPTER ONE

"This is so annoying!" Ionie looked at her friends in frustration as they sat in the clearing. "I hate that there's a mystery we haven't solved!"

Her Star Animal, Sorrel – a wildcat – swished her long tabby tail. "It's been over a week since we discovered that Shades were causing the strange events happening in the village and we still haven't found out who conjured them from the shadows."

"I know but we've all been busy," Lottie pointed out, cuddling Juniper, her red squirrel.

"We all had family things on at Easter so we couldn't meet up then."

"And after that I was on holiday," added Sita, her arm round Willow, her fallow deer.

"I was away for a few days, too," said Maia, pushing her blond fringe out of her eyes and kissing Bracken, her fox, on the nose.

"Well, now we're all back together, we can discover what's going on," said Ionie. "We've got six days until school starts. Hopefully that will be enough time to solve the mystery and stop whoever it is from conjuring Shades again."

Maia stroked Bracken's russet fur. Ionie was right: they had to work out what was going on. The week before last they had found some horrible Shades trapped in dolls in the house of an older couple, Ana and Mike Jefferson, who lived in the village. The Shades had been trying to make Mike's heart's desire – for Westcombe to win the contest for Best Kept Village – come true. The village had won the title, but the Shades' actions had upset everyone, including Mike. They'd stolen play equipment from gardens, dug up flower beds, cut down ivy on houses and locked up pet cats and the ducks from the pond. Luckily Maia and the others had tracked the Shades down and sent them back to the shadows.

"Should I see if the magic can give me any clues that might help?" Maia said, pulling a small mirror from her pocket. The others nodded eagerly.

They had all learned to use the magic current to do different types of magic. Maia could look into a shining surface and see things that were happening in other places. She could also look into the past and the future, and ask the magic to show her things that might help the Star Friends. Sometimes she had magic dreams that gave her important information.

Lottie could use the magic current to become very agile and she had recently developed the ability to sense when danger was approaching. Sita could heal wounds and command people to do whatever she wanted, although she didn't like making people obey her so she only used that power in emergencies. Ionie could travel to different places, using shadows, and she could cast glamours – disguising objects or people. She was also a Spirit Speaker, which meant that she could send Shades back to the shadows.

Maia took a deep breath. *Don't think about anything else, just think about the magic,* she told herself. She focused on the mirror and felt herself connect with the current. It always felt as if a door had opened in her mind, allowing the magic current to surge into her, tingling through her veins.

"Show me anything that will help us work out who put the Shades in the dolls," she breathed into the mirror.

Her own reflection faded and she saw a picture of the main road that led into the village – there was a row of houses and the Copper Kettle café. She had seen the same image when they were trying to find the Heart's Desire Shades. The image faded to be replaced by another picture she had seen previously – a small rectangular black object. Maia still couldn't tell what it was… Maybe a TV remote? Before she could get a good look, that image faded, too, and became a woman looking into a mirror with lights all around it. The woman in the mirror had red hair. Whenever she had seen the image before, Maia had always felt that there was something odd about it, but she could never work out what. Before she could figure it out, a new image appeared – a necklace made of multi-coloured beads with a large, silver pendant in the shape of an M. The pictures faded and Maia found herself staring at her own reflection again.

"Well?" Bracken asked as Maia looked up at them.

She reported what she'd seen. "I just keep seeing the same things – the main road by the

Copper Kettle, a TV remote and a woman looking in a mirror. Although there was one new picture – a necklace. I don't know what they all mean."

The others swapped uncertain looks.

"You used to also see Mike and Ana's house next to the ivy-covered cottage," said Ionie.

"I'm not seeing that any more," said Maia. "But I guess that's because we've got rid of the Shades who were in Ana's dolls."

"Well, this is no good," said Sorrel, getting up and stalking around. "Sitting here like day-old kittens won't solve the mystery – we need a plan of action. If the magic clues aren't helping, then I suggest we start by trying to find out if the people who own the dolls have any enemies."

"That makes sense," said Lottie. "After all, only someone who dislikes Ana and Mike would have put Shades in their dolls."

"But no one dislikes them," said Sita. Ana

was a school governor and Mike was chair on the school Parent Teacher Association and did a lot of fund-raising. They were very popular in the village.

"There *has* to be someone who doesn't like them for the Shades to have been put in Ana's dolls. Let's go and see if they're home," said Maia, getting to her feet.

"Yes, then come back and tell us what they said!" Bracken said eagerly, jumping up as well and almost knocking Sorrel over.

Sorrel's tail puffed up. "Watch it, fox!"

"You shouldn't be so slow, pussycat!" Bracken pounced on her tail and tweaked the hairs at the end of it with his teeth. "Got you!"

Sorrel swiped at him furiously with a paw. Bracken darted back, hiding behind Maia's legs. "Slowcoach!" he teased.

Sorrel hissed again.

"Just ignore him, Sorrel," Ionie said,

stroking the wildcat's head. Bracken often teased Sorrel and she always got cross. Sorrel rubbed her forehead against Ionie's hand and her fur flattened as she calmed down. She was sharp-tongued, but she adored Ionie.

"Right, off you go then," Juniper said to the girls, waving at them with his paw. "Call for us and tell us what you've found out as soon as you can."

"We will," they promised.

The animals vanished and would reappear as soon as the girls called their names.

"Off to Ana and Mike's then," said Lottie, turning a cartwheel on the soft grass.

Maia grinned. "To try to solve the mystery at last!"

CHAPTER TWO

The girls headed down the path that led out of the clearing, pushing the overgrown brambles out of the way. The path came out on a quiet, stony track opposite a pretty thatched cottage where Maia's Granny Anne used to live before she died. Maia had recently found out that her granny had been a Star Friend, too, and that her Star Animal had been a beautiful silver wolf.

She really wished her granny was still alive. It would have been amazing to do magic together and to talk about the Star World.

And not just that: more and more Maia felt she would like to talk to her granny about all the other things that were happening in her normal, non-magic life – the Year Six SATs exams that were coming up, her first long school trip when she would be away from home for four nights, and starting secondary school in September.

There were so many new things happening! It was a bit scary. But, she reminded herself, becoming a Star Friend had been a new thing once. Her life had changed hugely when she'd met Bracken and she would never wish to go back to how it had been before. Doing magic and being his Star Friend was amazing!

Maia and the others turned left on the track and headed up the hill towards the village. At the top of the track, beside the main road, there was a row of stone houses where Ionie lived with her mum and dad.

"Wait a sec," Ionie said. "Let me just ask Mum something."

She dashed inside and came out a few minutes later, grinning and waving a ten-pound note. "Mum gave me this so we can get ice creams from the Copper Kettle on our way!"

"Yum!" said Maia. The Copper Kettle had the best home-made ice cream ever!

They crossed over the busy main road at the top of the lane. The Copper Kettle was on the other side of the road. It had a large bay window and was very cosy inside, with an old-fashioned glass counter filled with cakes and pastries, and two large rooms with round tables and mismatched chairs. In the winter, a fire always burned in the grate, but now it was spring there was a large bunch of flowers in the fireplace, arranged inside an old copper kettle. Dried flowers and antique pans hung from the ceiling and there were shelves on the walls with displays of Victorian baby dolls and old-fashioned teddies. A hatstand stood beside the till and there was a wooden newspaper rack on the wall by the door. Mary, who ran the café, was an older lady with short brown hair and she lived in a flat above the café.

When the girls opened the door, they saw that Mary was sitting behind the counter, reading a magazine. There were no customers at the tables. "Hello, girls," she said. "What can I get you?"

"Ice creams, please," said Ionie.

They all chose what they would like – honeycomb for Maia, chocolate for Lottie, mint choc chip for Ionie and strawberries and cream for Sita.

"It's very quiet today," Ionie said, looking round at the empty café.

Mary sighed. "I've never known business to be so bad at this time of year. People used to stop here as they travelled down the coast, but now they seem to be driving on and heading for the new marina instead."

A few months ago, a marina had opened further along the coastal road – there was a water park, a hotel and a café.

"You should put a big sign up advertising your ice cream so people stop here instead," said Maia, licking her cone. "It's the best ice cream in the world!"

"It's my grandma's special recipe," said Mary, "made with just a touch of Cornish magic!" But, although she smiled, Maia could see the worry in her face. "I do hope things improve. If they don't, I may have to shut the café. I can't keep it going with no customers. I was hoping that winning Best Kept Village might help, but it hasn't."

"You can't close down," Lottie said in dismay. "We love coming here."

Mary smiled at them. "Well, if you think of any clever plans to drum up some more business then let me know."

"We will," Maia promised.

They said goodbye and left.

"I wish there was a way we could help Mary using magic," said Ionie.

"So do I," said Maia. "But I don't see how."

"I guess there are some things even magic can't help with," said Sita. "Like starting secondary school and SATs tests."

"And having a mum who makes you revise for them all the time," groaned Lottie. She glanced at Sita. "Though maybe you could command her not to?"

"No!" said Sita firmly. She sighed. "I hope the exams are going to be OK. I'm really worried about them."

"They'll be easy, don't stress," said Ionie airily. She was very clever.

Maia glanced at Sita. She didn't look convinced.

As they passed the duck pond on the village green, they discussed their plan. The girls decided that it might seem odd if they all turned up at Ana and Mike's and that it would be better if Maia went by herself.

"I'll ask if Lucia's in," said Maia. Lucia was Ana and Mike's little granddaughter. She was in Reception at school and Maia was her Year Six buddy. Maia left the others and went on alone to Ana and Mike's cottage. Mike was in the garden, doing some weeding, and Ana was chatting to him.

"Hi, Maia," said Ana as Maia opened the
gate. Ana was in her late fifties with dark hair.
She'd grown up in Portugal, but had lived
in Westcombe for many years. She and Mike
were moving to live in Portugal after the
summer. He was a bit older than Ana and was
very tall and slim with a broad smile.

"Hi!" Maia said. "Is Lucia with you today?"

Ana nodded. "She is and I'm sure she'd love
to see you. Lucia! Maia's here!" she called,

standing by the front door. "Come on in," she said, beckoning Maia inside.

Lucia ran down the stairs, her pigtails bobbing. "Maia!" she squealed. "Come and see the cookies I made with Nana!"

She grabbed Maia by the hand and pulled her into the kitchen. As they passed the dining room, Maia caught sight of Ana's collection of old-fashioned foreign dolls on the window ledge. A shiver ran down her spine. Last time she'd been in the house, the dolls had been possessed by Shades and they had attacked her and the others. They were just normal dolls again now, but Maia still found them creepy.

In the kitchen, a batch of cookies was cooling on the rack. "Would you two like to ice them with me?" Ana said, washing her hands.

"Yes, please," said Maia. It would be a great chance to get Ana talking.

They settled down at the table with spoons

and a bowl full of icing. As they began to ice the cookies, Maia tried to work out how she was going to ask Ana if there was anyone who might not like her and Mike. It was a bit of an odd question to just come out with!

"Can I have a cookie, Nana?" Lucia said.

"Yes, OK," said Ana with a smile. "Maia, do you want one?"

"Thanks but I'm full at the moment," said Maia. "I've just had an ice cream."

"From the Copper Kettle? Were there many people in there?" Ana asked.

"No, it was really quiet," said Maia.

"Poor Mary," sighed Ana. "It's such a shame that new marina went ahead. It's been bad for her business. Mike tried to oppose it when it was at the planning stage – he knew it would affect the shops here in Westcombe – but it went ahead anyway. Desmond Hannigan's disliked Mike ever since."

Maia's ears pricked up at the mention of

someone who didn't like Mike. "Desmond Hannigan? Who's he?"

"The owner of the marina," said Ana. She smiled. "Still, if in sixty years you've only made one enemy in life, then that's a life lived well as far as I'm concerned."

Maia stored the information in her head. So Mike only had one enemy and it was this Desmond Hannigan. Maybe he was responsible for putting the Shades in the dolls?

"The cookies are yummy, Nana," said Lucia, licking her fingers.

Ana smiled. "It's a recipe from Portugal."

"You made them for the PTA psychic evening that Mike organized, didn't you?" Maia remembered. "When that lady, Mystic Maureen, came and told people's fortunes?"

Ana nodded. "Yes, that was a great evening. It was actually Mary at the Copper Kettle who suggested it. She gave one of Mystic Maureen's business cards to Mike and it turned out to be a real fund-raiser. Look." She took a photo off the fridge and handed it to Maia.

Maia glanced at the photo. It showed Mystic Maureen and some of the parents with Mike. Maia remembered the fortune-teller well. She had shoulder-length red hair and was wearing a colourful dress and an unusual scarf.

She was about to hand the photo back when something caught her eye. Around Mystic Maureen's neck there was a necklace with a large pendant in the shape of an M.

Maia froze. It was the same necklace the

magic had shown her! She studied the photo more closely, remembering that the magic had also shown her someone sitting at a mirror. Excitement started to swirl inside her as she realized that the person she had seen in the mirror looked quite like Mystic Maureen!

Could Mystic Maureen have had something to do with the Shades in Ana's dolls? The timing fitted – the Shades had started to do things in the village just after the fortune-telling evening. And, now Maia thought about it, Mystic Maureen had seemed really interested in the dolls. She'd told Ana she collected dolls herself and had taken photos of Ana's with her phone. Thinking back, it was very suspicious.

"Are you OK, Maia?" Ana asked and Maia realized she was still staring at the photo.

"Yes, I'm fine," she said, handing it back. But inside she was more than fine, she was jumping up and down with excitement. She couldn't wait to tell the others what she had found out!

Chapter Three

Maia was almost bursting with her news by the time she left Ana's house. The others were waiting on the bench by the duck pond.

"You've discovered something, haven't you?" Sita asked, seeing her excited face.

"Yes! Listen to this!" Maia pulled them into a huddle and told them everything. "I think the magic was trying to tell me it was Mystic Maureen who put the Shades in the dolls," she finished. "I'm sure it was her looking in the mirror and it showed me her necklace, too."

"What about the other things it showed you
– the main road and the thing that looked like
a remote control?" said Lottie. "How do they
fit in?"

Maia shrugged impatiently. "I don't know,
but the important thing is that we find Mystic
Maureen!"

"So how do we do that?" said Ionie.

Maia remembered something. "Ana told me
that Mary gave Mike one of Mystic Maureen's
business cards. There must be some at the
Copper Kettle. If we can get one, it should
have a phone number or address on."

"The Copper Kettle!" Ionie exclaimed
suddenly. "You said the bit of road the magic
showed you had the Copper Kettle on and
Mystic Maureen's cards are in the Copper
Kettle. Maybe the magic was trying to tell you
that the Copper Kettle is important and we
should go there?"

"Yes! Let's go now!" said Maia.

"This is so good! We've finally got a suspect!" said Ionie as they set off. "I can't wait to tell Sorrel!"

"I wonder why Mystic Maureen would put Shades in the dolls," said Lottie.

"I have no idea," said Maia. "She seemed perfectly friendly with Mike and Ana that evening, and Ana's just told me that Mike has no enemies apart from a man called Desmond Hannigan who owns the new marina."

"We definitely need to question her and find out what's going on!" said Sita.

When the girls arrived at the Copper Kettle, there was no one inside.

"With you in a minute!" Mary's voice called from the kitchen.

Ionie went to the payment desk. Beside the till was a selection of flyers and local business cards. "I can't see any cards for

Mystic Maureen," she said.

Maia joined her. There were business cards for florists, pet sitters, plumbers and childminders, but none for Mystic Maureen.

"Hello, girls. Back again already!" They looked up as Mary came through from the kitchen area, dusting flour off her hands on to her apron. "I was just trying out a new recipe for cakes, another one from my grandma's recipe book. What can I get you then? More ice cream?"

Maia smiled. "No, thank you. Actually, we just came in to see if you have any business cards for Mystic Maureen, the fortune-teller?"

"Mystic Maureen?" Mary looked a bit surprised. "Goodness. Why do you want one of her cards?"

"She did a fund-raising evening for the PTA," Maia said. "My mum was there and asked me to pick up one of her cards," she fibbed.

"I think there were a few here, but," Mary had a look round the counter, "I'm afraid they all seem to have gone."

"Oh," said Ionie in disappointment.

"I don't suppose you know anything about her?" said Lottie hopefully. "Like where she lives?"

"Not really." Mary cleared her throat. "She's only been in a few times. I seem to remember she said she was based at the new marina, but I can't be sure. Now ... um ... if that's all, I'd really better get back to my baking!" She hurried to the kitchen.

The girls left the café and headed for the clearing to tell the animals what they'd found out.

"It's annoying that there weren't any of

Mystic Maureen's cards left," Ionie said in a low voice. "What are we going to do now?"

"We could look on the internet," Lottie suggested. "She may have a website." She pulled out her phone. "I'll put in Mystic Maureen, fortune-teller, Devon." There was a pause and then her forehead furrowed. "Nothing."

"Maybe you're spelling her name wrong?" said Sita.

Lottie tried again with different spellings. "No, still nothing," she said after a few more attempts. "No mention of her at all."

"Then I guess she doesn't have a website," suggested Sita.

"Mary said she thinks she's based at the marina. How about we go there tomorrow morning and see if we can find her?" said Ionie. "It's too late now. Maia's mum will start to wonder where we are if we don't go back soon."

They were having a sleepover at Maia's that night.

"We could go to the marina after breakfast," Maia suggested.

"We'll need someone to give us a lift," Lottie pointed out.

"We don't need anyone to drive us," Ionie said. She looked at their confused faces and grinned. "I can shadow-travel us all there!"

As the girls walked back to Maia's house, they decided that after breakfast the next day they would say they were going for a walk, then run to the clearing where Ionie would use her magic to take them to the marina.

"Hi, girls," Maia's dad said, appearing in the kitchen doorway as they arrived at Maia's house. He had an apron on and his hands were floury. "I'm making home-made pizzas. Do you want to come and choose toppings?"

They shrugged off their coats and shoes and headed into the kitchen. Alfie, Maia's little brother, was in his high chair, making shapes with bits of leftover dough, while Mrs Greene, Maia's mum, and Clio, Maia's fifteen-year-old sister, were washing up. The girls set to work, getting the toppings ready to put on the pizzas.

"Do you remember your eighth birthday party, Lottie, when you had a pizza-making party?" Sita said as she grated cheese.

"It was really funny," Lottie said to Ionie, who hadn't been friends with her then. "We went to a pizza restaurant and this chef was showing us how to stretch pizza dough. I tried to swirl mine round and it flew out of my hands and went all over him!"

Maia's dad chuckled. "You've all had some fun birthday parties. You had a magician for your fifth birthday party, didn't you, Ionie?'

Maia grinned. "I remember that. You kept getting cross with him because you said he wasn't doing the magic properly."

"Well, he wasn't!" said Ionie. "I could see the rabbit behind his table and the scarf stuffed up his sleeve!"

"It's strange to think that next year you might be having birthday parties with people you don't know – new friends from your secondary schools," said Mrs Greene.

"We'll still have our old friends, too," Maia replied quickly. She knew Lottie and Sita were both a bit anxious about starting secondary, but for different reasons. Lottie was worried about them staying friends because she was going to a different secondary school to the others. She was going to the all-girls high school whereas they were going to King John's – the local academy. Sita was nervous because she didn't like anything changing. She didn't even like it when they changed classes every year so the thought of starting a new school was very worrying.

Sita sighed. "I just know I'm going to get lost when we start at King John's. I wish we could stay at Westcombe forever."

"I don't," said Ionie. "I'm looking forward to changing schools. The science labs at King John's look amazing!"

"My school has a maths club and runs a maths Olympiad and maths competitions," said Lottie. "How cool is that?"

"Awesome!' said Ionie.

"You two are seriously weird," said Maia with a grin. Both Ionie and Lottie were very clever and loved competitions. She looked across at Sita and remembered what she'd been thinking about earlier. "Changing schools will be fine," she said. "Just because something's new and different doesn't mean it's going to be bad." She wished she could remind Sita that being a Star Friend had been a new thing for them last year, but she couldn't say that in front of her family.

"Mmm," Sita said, not sounding convinced.

"Maia's right, Sita," said Clio, coming over. "I know it feels like a really big deal but you get used to it very quickly. All the new Year Sevens are assigned older buddies to help them find their way round for the first few weeks, so don't worry about getting lost, and the teachers will be nice to you – well, at first!"

Mrs Greene nodded. "I'm sure after a few weeks you'll wonder why you were ever worried," she said.

"I'm ready to cook the pizzas!" said Mr Greene. "Time to choose your toppings!"

They all started piling on the toppings. As Maia arranged pepperoni, sweetcorn and peppers on hers, she pushed all thoughts of school out of her head. Right now, she was happy exactly where she was – getting ready for a home-made pizza feast with her friends and family, and having a fun magic adventure to look forward to in the morning!

Chapter Four

By nine o'clock that night, the girls were
snuggled up in their sleeping bags in Maia's
bedroom with their animals.

"I can't wait until the morning," said Ionie,
stroking Sorrel, who was stretched out beside
her, purring happily. "I hope we track down
Mystic Maureen so we can find out more
about the dolls and why she put the Shades in
them."

"Be careful," said Willow. She was beside
Sita, her slender legs curled underneath her.

"If this fortune-teller is the one doing dark magic, she might be dangerous."

"I wish we could come with you," said Bracken, nestling in Maia's bed to get closer to her.

She stroked his ears. "I know, but I think people might ask questions if we arrived at the marina with a fox, a wildcat, a squirrel and a deer!"

Juniper looked up from Lottie's pillow. "I hope you manage to solve the mystery of the Shades."

Maia felt a shiver of excitement run through her. She was really hoping that, too!

Maia felt like she had only just drifted off to sleep when she found herself in a vivid dream. Mystic Maureen was sitting at a table, peering at an old-fashioned phone, and Maia was standing behind her. On the phone screen she could see a picture of one of Ana's dolls.

"You *did* do it!" Maia said to her. "You put the Shades in the dolls!"

But Mystic Maureen didn't hear her. "It'll help," she whispered to herself. "I'm sure it will."

What did she mean? Maia frowned but just then she heard angry voices, shouting and banging. She turned. There was a doorway behind her. People were hammering on it and yelling. What was going on? They sounded furious.

The door started to splinter and Maia turned to run…

Maia sat up in bed. The sky outside was still dark.

"Maia?" Bracken said.

"I was having a weird dream," she whispered, not wanting to disturb the others.

"A magic dream?" Bracken said with concern.

"I think so." Maia rubbed her forehead. "Mystic Maureen was in it. She was looking at a photo of one of Ana's dolls on her phone. When she was at Ana's house for the fortune-telling evening, I saw her taking photos of the dolls. It was a bit weird."

"Was there anything else in your dream?" Bracken asked.

"Yes. There was a door and there were people on the other side of it trying to get through – they sounded angry."

Bracken looked concerned. "I wonder what that means."

"I don't know but it was quite frightening," said Maia uneasily.

"The sooner you find this Mystic Maureen, the better," Bracken said, licking her hand comfortingly.

Maia hugged him. She was sure Mystic Maureen was the person who had conjured the Shades. They had to find her and stop her as soon as possible, and definitely before she used dark magic again. An image of the people hammering on the door flashed back into her mind. Maybe that would actually happen if they didn't find Mystic Maureen in time...

The next morning, the girls had a quick breakfast and told Mrs Greene they were going out. They raced to the clearing and gathered under a tree. Maia had shadow-travelled quite a few times with Ionie but it always felt weird. One minute she was standing in the shadows beside a tree with the others and the next she felt the world slide away. It was like travelling in a very fast lift. A second later, her feet hit tarmac and the four of them were now standing in a small alleyway.

At the end of the alleyway they could see people walking past on a sunny street. There were babies in buggies, small children with fishing nets and adults carrying beach towels. People's voices travelled towards them but no one glanced in their direction.

"Time to find Mystic Maureen!" Ionie said. "Come on!"

The others followed her out of the alley.

Seagulls were swooping across the blue sky and the air smelled of seaweed and frying onions. On the other side of the wide street there was a harbour with moored boats, their sails folded. Further along the street there were some souvenir and clothes shops, a small supermarket and at the far end was a smart hotel with a large café beside it. The girls walked along the busy street, looking at all the shops and businesses. Then they checked the harbour where people were selling hot dogs and offering face-painting and hair-braiding. Finally they reached the café.

"Maybe Mary got it wrong," Maia said, puzzled. "I thought we'd find a fortune-telling hut or something like that, but there's no sign of Mystic Maureen anywhere."

"Why don't we go and get an ice cream from the café?" said Lottie. "I've got some money with me. We could ask the waiting staff there if they've heard of Mystic Maureen."

They went into the bustling Friendly Fish café. The staff inside were rushed off their feet serving people. The girls queued up for ice-cream cones. When it was their turn to be served, Maia asked the waitress if she had heard of someone called Mystic Maureen. "She's a fortune-teller," she added.

"I've never heard of anyone of that name," said the woman as she made up their cones. "But if it's a fortune-teller you want then you should come back tomorrow." She handed out the ice creams.

They took them and squeezed round a small table beside the counter. "I wonder what she meant about coming back tomorrow?" Maia asked but she was interrupted by the sound of a raised voice behind them.

A cross-looking man was telling off two of the waitresses. He had slicked-back grey hair and round eyes like a fish. "People are only allowed ketchup if they pay for it," he was saying sharply. "The same goes for mayonnaise. No freebies. Do you understand?"

"Yes, Mr Hannigan," muttered the waitresses.

Maia stiffened. Hannigan? Where had she heard that name before?

"This place is really busy, isn't it?" said Sita.

"I don't know why," said Ionie, wrinkling

her nose. "This ice cream is nowhere near as good as Mary's. It tastes really artificial and," she half stood up to peer at the counter, "those cakes look like they've been there for a few days."

The man scolding the waitresses overheard her. "I'll have you know that all our cakes here at the Friendly Fish café are freshly made!" he said.

"Well, your ice cream doesn't taste very nice." Ionie loved an argument and pointed to a sign by the ice-cream counter. "Is it really home-made? It doesn't taste like it is."

The man's eyes bulged angrily. "What?"

Maia noticed that people around them had started to listen in. Ionie seemed to have noticed, too.

"The Copper Kettle's ice cream is much better," she said loudly.

Maia hid a grin. She knew exactly what Ionie was doing. Maybe the people who heard her would now try Mary's cafe instead!

"Absolute rubbish! Now get out of here! You can't take up a table if you're just having ice cream anyway. Tables are for meals only!" snapped the man.

"Come on, Ionie," said Sita, who hated scenes and shouting.

"Fine, we'll go. We'll just head on back to THE COPPER KETTLE!" Ionie said, almost shouting the name. "They're very friendly there!"

"Ionie!" Sita exclaimed to Ionie as they left. "That man was really angry with you."

"So?" said Ionie.

"He was mean," said Lottie.

Maia suddenly remembered where she had heard the man's name before. "I know who he is! He's the person who doesn't like Mike – Desmond Hannigan. He owns the marina."

"If he doesn't like Mike, he's definitely a horrible person," said Lottie. "Mike's really nice. I suppose Mr Hannigan could be a suspect," she went on. "He could have put the Shades in the dolls."

Maia pictured Mr Hannigan. He really hadn't looked like the kind of person who would do magic. "Mystic Maureen seems much more likely. I saw her with the dolls and the magic hasn't shown me Mr Hannigan at all."

"I guess that's true," Lottie conceded.

"If only we could find her!" said Maia. She went to put the remains of her cone in a nearby bin. As she did so, she saw a poster stuck to a noticeboard:

Psychic Fair and Holistic Therapies
15th April 10 a.m.–4 p.m.
The Grand Hotel
Stockwood Marina

❀

Crystal healing, chakra balancing,

aura reading and fortune tellings.

Come and balance your body,

soothe your mind and discover your future.

❀

£10 per person – No concessions and

no admittance to children under 14.

❀

Maia gasped. The 15th April was the following day! That must have been what the waitress meant when she said they should come back tomorrow if they wanted a fortune-teller.

"Look!" She pointed to the notice.

"We've got to go!" said Ionie. "If it's a psychic fair with fortune-telling, Mystic Maureen will probably be there."

"But it's really expensive and it says you have to be fourteen," said Sita.

Maia thought for a moment. She certainly didn't have ten pounds and none of them looked fourteen so even if Ionie shadow-travelled them inside they'd probably be asked to leave.

Ionie chuckled suddenly. "Hang on, I think I might just have an idea!" she said, her green eyes shining. "How about—"

"Ionie!" squeaked Lottie in alarm, pointing behind her. "It's your dad!"

Ionie's dad was heading down the street towards them. He was skirting round a group of parents with toddlers and hadn't noticed them yet. "Quick! We're not supposed to be at the marina. Hide!" Maia gasped.

CHAPTER FIVE

The girls dived into a nearby souvenir shop and watched from inside as Ionie's dad walked down the street.

"We'd better go home in case he sees us," said Maia. "Come on – quick! While he's heading the other way!"

They hurried to the alley and stepped into the shadows beside the bins.

"I'll take us back to the clearing," said Ionie. "We can call the animals and I'll tell you my idea for tomorrow. Hold hands!"

They grabbed hands. The alley vanished into shadows and they were swept away.

As their feet touched solid ground, Maia breathed in the earthy smell of trees and leaves. Birds twittered in the branches and a wild grey squirrel was looking down at them curiously from a tree.

They called their animals' names. Within the blink of an eye, the four Star Animals appeared. Bracken and Juniper bounded into Maia and Lottie's arms. Willow cantered playfully round the clearing and Sorrel wove round Ionie's legs, purring loudly. After they had all said hello, the girls sat down by the waterfall and told the animals everything that had happened.

"So, we might not have found Mystic Maureen today, but Ionie's got an idea for how we can get into the fortune-telling fair tomorrow," finished Maia.

"It isn't how we can get in, but how I can get in," said Ionie. "Watch."

The air shimmered around her and
suddenly she changed into an old lady with
grey hair in a bun and deep wrinkles around
her mouth and eyes. She was wearing a long
red skirt and had a black shawl round her
shoulders. She rubbed her hands together.
"Who'd like Psychic Susan to do a reading for
them at the fair tomorrow? Would you, my
dear?" She shuffled over to Maia. "Show me
your palm and I'll tell you your future!"

Maia squealed in delight. "Ionie! That's
brilliant!"

Sorrel purred like she was going to explode. "Oh, you excellent girl!" she said. "What a genius use of your magic!"

"You're really planning on going to the fair and pretending to be a fortune-teller?" said Sita, wide-eyed.

Ionie/Psychic Susan nodded. "I've been practising disguising myself using a glamour and now I can put it to good use," she said in her normal voice.

"But what if the disguise fails and that Mr Hannigan is there at the hotel and sees you?" said Lottie.

"It won't fail," Ionie said confidently. She transformed back into herself. "So, what do you think?"

"I think it's perfect!" said Maia, high-fiving her. Lottie and Sita were looking slightly worried, but Maia just felt envious. "I wish I could come with you."

"You can watch me using your own magic

and tell the others what's happening," said
Ionie. She beamed. "Let's meet here in the
morning and I'll shadow-travel there then.
Agreed?"

"Agreed!" they all said.

However, later that day, there was a change
of plan. Maia and Alfie were playing with his
trains on the kitchen floor when her phone
pinged. It was a message from Ionie to them all.

Hi. Dad was at the marina today cos he wanted
2 have a look around and see what it was like.
He says he'll take us all 2moro if we want to go.
I think we can still do what we were planning!
Ixxx

Maia smiled. The girls tried to be very
careful what they put in messages in case any
of their parents ever looked at their phones.

"Mum, can I go to the new marina with
Ionie and the others tomorrow?" she asked,

looking up. "Ionie's dad is going to take us."

"Sure," her mum said.

Maia texted Ionie back.

> I can come! What time? xx

> Dad says he'll pick u up at 9.30! Bring cossies and towels cos we're going 2 go 2 the water park. Fun and you-know-what! Ix

You-know-what was their code for magic. Maia sent Ionie smiley and winky faces back.

Just then the door opened and her dad and Clio came in. "Look what we picked up at the Copper Kettle!" he said. "Chocolate cake!" He opened the cake box to reveal a cake covered with chocolate fudge icing.

"Mmm," said Maia, her mouth watering. It looked delicious.

"I thought we could have it for pudding tonight," her dad said.

"I can't. I'm trying to be more healthy," said Clio.

"Just a little piece," Dad said, waving the

cake temptingly under her nose.

Clio groaned. "Don't be mean, Dad!"

"Cake!" Alfie said, looking up. "Want cake!"

Maia's mum smiled. "All right, you can have a bit of cake, then it's teeth and bed."

She cut a little slice. Alfie ate it greedily. "More!" His eyes widened. "Pleeeeease!"

"Just a tiny bit." Maia's mum handed him a second piece and licked her fingers. "It is rather good."

"It's a new recipe," said Maia, using her finger to pick up a few crumbs of sponge and icing from the box. It really was delicious.

"Want more cake! More!" Alfie cried.

Mr Greene laughed. "No more now, Alfie. It's bedtime."

Alfie started to kick and scream as his dad picked him up. "Oh dear," said Maia's mum, rolling her eyes at the girls as Alfie was carried out of the kitchen. "I think someone's rather overtired tonight. Now let's set the table for supper."

As Maia got out the cutlery, she thought about the next day. Hopefully they would get to meet Mystic Maureen. She felt a flutter of excitement. Maybe tomorrow they were finally going to get some real answers!

Chapter Six

The next morning, Ionie's dad drove them all to the marina. "Who's ready to go in the swimming pool?" he said as they parked and got out.

"Actually, Dad, could we shop a bit first?" asked Ionie.

"Sure," her dad said. "If you want to have a mooch around, I'll go to the café. See you in a bit!" And he left them to it.

"OK, this is my chance," hissed Ionie when he was gone. "I'll go into the changing room in one of the shops, disguise myself and then shadow-travel into the fair at the hotel."

"Meanwhile we'll watch you with my magic!" Maia said.

"Don't do anything dangerous!" said Lottie.

Ionie grinned. "Me? Never!" She winked at them and headed into a nearby clothes shop.

The others found a bench in a quiet spot by the harbour wall, away from all the crowds and from Ionie's dad. Maia cradled the mirror in her hands. "Show me Ionie," she said.

As she connected with the magic, the surface of the mirror glimmered and an image of a lady with grey hair, a long red skirt and a black shawl round her shoulders appeared. Only her green eyes were recognizably Ionie's. "I can see her! She looks amazing," Maia told the others.

"Where is she?" asked Lottie.

"In a big room inside the hotel," Maia answered, her eyes scanning the picture.

"It's a got a high ceiling and quite a lot of people inside. There are people sitting behind tables, selling things." Maia read a few of the signs propped up on the tables: aura reading, mystical books, moon-blessed herbs...

A shiver ran down her spine as she read that sign. She knew it was possible for people to learn how to harness the power in plants and herbs to do magic. Some people used that kind of magic to do good, but she and the others had once had to stop someone evil who was using plant magic to upset people.

"What's Ionie doing?" asked Sita anxiously.

"She's just walking around." Maia could tell Ionie was enjoying being in disguise. She was smiling at people, nodding and stopping to chat to some of the stallholders.

A girl of about eighteen with pink hair came up to her and asked her something. Maia focused on the picture in the mirror until she could hear what was being said.

"So you're really a fortune-teller?" the girl was saying to Ionie.

"Yes, my dear," Ionie replied. "I can pull back the veil of the future and see beyond it to what will come."

Maia grinned.

The girl's eyes widened. "Will you look into my future?"

Ionie took the girl's hand and stared at it for a long moment. "Elephants!" she announced suddenly. "I see elephants in your future!"

Maia started to giggle. What was Ionie doing?

"Elephants?" echoed the girl. "Wow! That's so weird. I love elephants. How did you know?"

"Magic," said Ionie, but Maia saw her eyes flick to the silver elephant necklace and earrings the girl was wearing. "You must travel far to see them and you will do a lot of good!"

"That's awesome! I've been trying to decide where to go on my gap year before uni. Now I know!" said the girl. "I'll go to Sri Lanka and help at an elephant orphanage. Thank you so much!" She hurried off, smiling. Ionie hid a grin.

"What's happening?" said Sita as Maia chuckled.

"Ionie's having fun." Maia told them about the girl, while still keeping an eye on Ionie, who was now talking to one of the fortune-tellers sitting behind a table. "She's heading for the door now," she said, watching as Ionie left. "She's going down a corridor. I think she's looking for somewhere she can go to travel back." She saw Ionie look around and check she was alone before stepping into a patch of shadows and vanishing. "Yes, she's coming back!"

"Let's go and meet her," said Sita.

They reached the shop just as Ionie came out. "That was so much fun!" She grabbed Maia's hands in excitement.

"Excuse me, what do you think you're doing?" They all swung round at the sound of Ionie's dad's voice. He walked over, frowning. "Please leave these girls alone."

Ionie had been in such a rush she'd forgotten to change back into herself! To Maia's horror, Ionie didn't hurry off. She just ducked her head so her dad couldn't see her eyes and grabbed his hand. "I could read your fortune, kind sir. Psychic Sue is never wrong."

"Um… Er…" Mr Cooper looked like he didn't know what to do.

"Aha, I see you have a very clever daughter with red hair," said Ionie in her croaky old-lady voice. "Yes, I can see her here in your palm. She is very clever indeed and she deserves more pocket money."

Mr Cooper blinked. "What?"

"I really think you should go now, Psychic Sue," said Maia hastily as Lottie tried to hold back her laughter and snorted loudly.

"I will be back," declared Ionie. "Mark my words! And remember, Psychic Sue is never wrong!" With that, she hurried away, disappearing into the crowd of people on the streets.

Mr Cooper shook his head. "What an eccentric woman!" He looked round. "Where's Ionie, girls?"

"Um, quite near," said Lottie truthfully.

"I think she went into one of the shops to try something on," said Sita.

Just then Ionie came jogging over, looking like her usual eleven-year-old self. "Here she is!" Maia said.

Ionie skipped over to them. "Thanks for waiting for me! Hi, Dad."

"Ionie, I don't want you going off on your

own," said her dad. "There are some very strange people about."

"Really?" said Ionie innocently. "OK, we'll stick together from now on."

"Let's get your swimming things and go to the water park," said her dad.

They followed him back to the car. "What did you find out at the fair?" Maia asked quietly.

"I'll tell you when we're on our own," Ionie whispered back.

They had to wait until they were in the girls' changing rooms before they were alone. They huddled together in a single cubicle. "I can't believe you tried to tell your dad's fortune!" Sita whispered to Ionie.

"I know! Did you see his face?" Ionie grinned.

"It was very funny!" Maia said.

"Did you find out anything about Mystic

Maureen?" Lottie demanded.

"Well, she wasn't there and none of the other fortune-tellers had ever heard of her," said Ionie. "The last lady I spoke to said she knew everyone in the area who worked as a fortune-teller and she'd never heard of a Mystic Maureen."

"How weird!" said Maia.

Lottie looked thoughtful. "Unless Mystic Maureen isn't a real fortune-teller. Maybe she was just pretending for the PTA night?"

They considered that but then Ionie shook her head. "No, if that was the case, why would she have business cards at the Copper Kettle?"

"True," Lottie admitted.

"So what do we do now?" said Maia. "My dreams and magic visions are all telling me that Mystic Maureen put the Shades in Ana's dolls and hinting that something else bad is going to happen, but how do we find her?"

None of them knew.

"This is making my head hurt," groaned Sita. "I vote we go swimming and forget about it for a while."

The water park was lots of fun with twisting slides, a wave machine and warm tropical pools. Afterwards they had a picnic lunch and then played rounders on the beach. It was almost a relief just to be normal and to forget about the mystery of Mystic Maureen but when Maia was in her bedroom that night she talked about it with Bracken.

"I just don't get it," she said as they lay on her bed. "Why has no one heard of Mystic Maureen? It's like she's just vanished into thin air."

"It is very strange." He put his head on her tummy.

"Don't!" she said with a groan. "I ate too much for tea."

Her mum had been back to the Copper
Kettle and come home with a lemon drizzle
cake. The lemon drizzle had been just as
delicious as the chocolate cake – soft sponge
oozing with sweet lemon icing. Maia had had
three big slices and now she was feeling quite
sick!

Bracken rolled over on to
his back. Maia tickled
his belly. "I don't
know what else
we can do to
find her."

Her
phone
buzzed and
she picked
it up. There
was a group
message from
Lottie.

"Listen to this," Maia breathed. She read the message to Bracken. *"I've just had one of my weird feelings again! I was falling asleep when I suddenly felt scared, like something horrible was going to happen. This is just like last time when the Shades appeared. Something dangerous is coming. I know it."*

"That's not good," Bracken said anxiously. "Do you think more Shades are going to appear in Westcombe?"

Maia thought about the dream she'd had about the furious people trying to break a door down. Shades made people angry and behave in strange ways. "Maybe." She texted Lottie and the others back.

> We need 2 be careful. Let's meet 2moro and decide what 2 do then. Mxx

> OK. About 10? Sxx

> I can't. I'm out in the morning with Mum. Ix

> I've got a tennis lesson in the morning, too. How about we meet at 2 p.m. in the clearing? Lxx

Maia typed back.

> OK. But u and I cd meet earlier, Sita? We cd meet at mine and go 2 the clearing?

Sita sent a smiley face and a thumbs up back.

> Don't do ANYTHING without us!!!!! lxxx

> We won't. Night! Mxx

She put her phone down. "We're all going to meet tomorrow afternoon," she told Bracken.

"Good," said Bracken. "Then we can come up with a plan about what to do next."

Maia nodded and yawned. "I really hope I don't have bad dreams tonight," she said, flopping back against the pillow.

He snuggled closer. "I'll be here if you do."

She kissed his nose and fell asleep with him curled up in her arms.

CHAPTER SEVEN

To Maia's relief, all she dreamed about was cake. She was sitting in the Copper Kettle, eating one cake after another. It was much better than dreaming about Shades! She woke up, her tummy rumbling.

"After last night, I thought I wouldn't want to eat again for a whole day," she said to Bracken as she got up. "But I'm really hungry now! I'm going to get some breakfast."

However, once she was downstairs, she

couldn't find anything that appealed to her. Not cereal, not porridge, not toast. She shut the cupboard door with a bang.

"Are you OK?" her dad asked.

"I don't know what I want to eat," she said.

"I'm feeling like that, too," he admitted. "How about I make bacon and eggs?"

Maia loved cooked breakfasts so she nodded.

Her dad made the fry-up but when Maia started eating it she quickly lost her appetite. She ate half the plateful and then put her knife and fork down. "Sorry, I guess I'm not that hungry, Dad."

"Don't worry." Her dad was pushing his food unenthusiastically round his plate. "I thought I wanted this but now I'm not so sure. Maybe we're both coming down with something."

Maia nodded and, after putting her plate
in the dishwasher, went back upstairs, feeling
strangely grumpy.

At ten o'clock, Sita arrived and they headed for
the clearing, talking about the strange feeling
Lottie had had the night before.

"Do you think it means more Shades are
going to appear?" Sita asked anxiously.

"I don't know," said Maia. "We may be in

danger from some other type of dark magic."

She saw the worried expression on Sita's face and squeezed her arm. "It'll be OK. We've fought people using dark magic before and we've always won."

Sita nodded. "I'm so glad we're Star Friends and get to do magic together."

"I know," said Maia. "I was thinking the other day how much everything has changed since we found out about the Star World." She shot Sita a sideways look, seeing a chance to reassure her about starting school. "Change doesn't have to be bad, you know. New things can be good – really good! Like learning how to do magic."

Sita was quiet for a moment. "I hadn't thought about it like that before," she admitted.

"Imagine if we'd never met the Star Animals and our lives had stayed just like they were before we met them," Maia went on. "There's no way you would want that, is there?"

Sita shook her head firmly. "No! Being a Star Friend is the best thing that's ever happened to me. I couldn't bear to be without Willow now."

Maia felt the same about Bracken. "So, you see, change can be good," she said.

Sita nodded. "I guess." She glanced at her friend. "Are you worried about the SATs?"

"Kind of," Maia admitted. "Mum and Dad say they don't mind how I do as long as I try my best, but Clio did well in hers and I don't want to mess them up."

"A whole week of exams!" said Sita. "It's going to be horrible."

"Let's not think about it now," said Maia as they turned on to the main road. "The Copper Kettle looks busy today," she said. "There are loads of people inside."

She could see a queue of people at the counter. Mary and her assistant, Rebecca, were hurrying about, delivering food and quickly clearing up as people left so others could sit down.

"I bet it's because of the new cakes!" said Maia, feeling really pleased for Mary. "We had one last night and they're so yummy." She felt in her pocket. Her mum had given her some pocket money the day before. "I've got enough for a slice each. Shall we go in?"

"OK," said Sita eagerly. "I had some of the new cake yesterday. My gran brought a Victoria sponge round to our house for tea."

"You have to try the chocolate cake – and the lemon drizzle," said Maia. "They're amazing!"

They went in and joined the queue.

"The cakes in here are just so delicious," Maia heard a woman at a nearby table say. "So much better than the ones at the Friendly Fish."

"Yes," her companion said. "I heard people talking about them at the marina yesterday and thought I had to come and try them out."

She scraped the crumbs off her plate with her fork. "I'm going to be taking some home, that's for sure!"

Maia felt a warm glow. She was really pleased that people were realizing how much nicer Mary's cakes were than those at the marina café. Maybe Ionie's little outburst yesterday had worked! Desmond Hannigan wouldn't be pleased...

"Excuse me! Can we get another slice of carrot cake over here!" a man called, holding his hand in the air.

"With you in a minute!" Mary called back, looking flustered as she rang up a customer's bill. "Sorry about the wait," she apologized to the long queue of people standing at the counter. "I'll just be one moment."

"Coffee and walnut cake, three carrot cakes and a scone?" called Rebecca, coming through from the kitchen.

"That's for us!" called Margaret, one of Maia's granny's old friends who was sitting at a table with a group of ladies from church.

"They really do need to get more staff in here," the woman in front of Maia muttered.

"We could offer to help?" Maia said to Sita.

Sita nodded. "Yes, sure!"

Mary was delighted with the offer. "Thank you, girls. I could really do with some help cleaning tables and carrying plates. Rebecca and I are run off our feet!"

"We're free all morning," said Maia. "Just tell us what you want us to do."

The girls washed their hands in the kitchen and then set to work. Everyone certainly seemed to be enjoying the food.

"It's great you've got so many people in," Maia said to Mary as she helped her bring some new cakes through from the kitchen and put them under the counter.

Mary picked up a battered leather book from the side. "It's all thanks to Grandma's special recipes in here!"

There was a crash on the other side of the counter. Maia and Mary looked round. A man sitting at a nearby table had stood up and knocked his chair into Sita as she'd been passing with a plate of cake. Maia had noticed him earlier because he'd been behaving a bit strangely. He had kept a hat on that hid his face and he'd been taking pictures of the menu on his phone. He'd also been eating ice cream, which she had thought was a bit odd for a cold and grey morning.

"I'm sorry!" Sita gasped, looking at the mess on the floor. "I didn't realize you were about to stand up."

"You clearly weren't looking where you were going!" the man snapped. His voice sounded familiar.

"Don't worry, Sita," said Mary. "Are you OK, sir? Did any cake get on you? Do you need a cloth?" But the man had left some money on the table and was already hurrying out of the café.

When he was outside, he looked back and Maia realized who he was. Desmond Hannigan! But what was he doing in the Copper Kettle and why had he been acting so peculiarly? He hurried away and got into a shiny black car.

Maia set about clearing the table, her mind turning over the fact that Desmond Hannigan had been there. He didn't seem like the kind of person who would just call into the Copper Kettle for an ice cream. A niggling thought wormed its way into her mind. Their other magic adventures had taught her to take notice when people behaved strangely and this certainly seemed strange! Could Desmond Hannigan possibly have something to do with the dark magic after all? The magic hadn't shown her any pictures of him and he didn't look like the sort of person who would do magic. But he didn't like Mike, and the Star Friends had been tricked by people before.

No, she thought. *Surely Mystic Maureen has to be responsible.*

She picked up a newspaper from a table and put it in the wooden rack beside the door. As she did so, she spotted a multicoloured scarf hanging on the hatstand. She caught her breath. It was the same scarf Mystic Maureen had been wearing the night of the fortune-telling event! She swung round. Was Mystic Maureen here right now?

Heart beating fast, Maia studied all the people in the café. But there was no one who looked anything like the fortune-teller.

"Are you OK?" Mary said, pausing beside her.

Maia realized she must look odd, staring around wildly. "Yes, I'm... I'm fine," she said and hurried off to clean another table. But her mind was racing. Mystic Maureen must have been in the café and left her scarf there. If that was the case, then hopefully she'd come back and get it soon! *Then we'll finally get the chance to talk to her,* Maia thought.

Chapter Eight

Maia and Sita helped until it was time to meet the others. Mary had made them a sandwich for lunch and she gave them a large slice of carrot cake each to take away. To Maia's disappointment, Mystic Maureen hadn't come back to claim her scarf.

They ate their cake as they walked to the clearing to meet the others. Seeing Ionie and Lottie just ahead of them on the lane, they hurried to catch up.

"Hi!" called Lottie. "What have you two

been up to?"

"Helping at the Copper Kettle and eating cake." Maia grinned as she saw the surprise on Lottie and Ionie's faces. "We'll tell you all about it when we've got the animals, too. I think I might have found something that will help us track down Mystic Maureen!"

When they were in the clearing with their animals, Maia told them about the scarf.

"Mystic Maureen must have been in there," she finished. "And if she left her scarf there she's hopefully going to go back."

"We have to keep watch at the café for her!" Ionie said.

Juniper flicked his bushy tail. "I wonder if she has anything to do with the feeling Lottie had last night that danger is heading our way."

"Indeed," Sorrel said, rubbing her head against Ionie's fingers. "Maia, did you dream about anything last night?"

"Just eating cake in the Copper Kettle,"

Maia said. "No Shades. Nothing magic."

"The Copper Kettle again." Sorrel sat down thoughtfully and flicked her tail round her paws. "Maybe the new danger is going to appear there? After all, the scarf does suggest that the fortune-teller has visited the café recently."

"She could have left an object in there with a Shade inside it," said Juniper. "Maybe even that scarf itself!"

"Did you see anything unusual in the café this morning?" asked Bracken.

"No," said Sita. "Nothing. There were just lots of customers."

"There was one thing," Maia remembered. "Desmond Hannigan was there."

"The man who owns the marina?" said Lottie. "The man who was telling off those waitresses yesterday?"

"Yes," answered Maia. "And the man who doesn't like Mike. He was in the Copper Kettle this morning acting really strangely."

"What was he doing?" asked Willow curiously.

"He had his face hidden as if he didn't want to be recognized and he was taking photos of the menu," said Maia.

"He left really quickly," said Sita. "He made me drop some cake! What a waste!" She sighed. "You know, I wouldn't mind some more of Mary's cake right now."

"Me too," said Maia, her tummy rumbling at the thought.

"You've both just had some!" said Ionie.

"I know but it's so yummy," said Maia, thinking wistfully of the carrot cake.

"We have far more important things to think about than cake!" Sorrel said sharply. "What you've told us isn't much to go on. Maybe this man—"

"Wait!" Lottie exclaimed. Sorrel swished her tail, looking put out at being interrupted. "What did you just say, Sita? A few minutes ago. When Sorrel asked if there was anything unusual at the café, you said no, just lots of customers. Don't you see?" She looked round at them all. "That's something unusual! The Copper Kettle hasn't had many customers and then suddenly it's really busy? Maybe Mystic Maureen has put more Heart's Desire Shades somewhere in the café and they're granting Mary's wish for more customers, just like they granted Mike's wish that Westcombe would win the Best Kept Village competition."

"Brilliant idea, Lottie!" burst out Juniper.

"Yes! You could be right! Shades could be making people come in and eat Mary's food!" Sita exclaimed.

Sorrel spluttered. "Don't be ridiculous, girl! Shades make people angry, jealous, unhappy and scared – they do not make people want to eat cake! If Shades were involved, I think we'd see something rather more dramatic happening."

Sita's face fell. "Oh."

Willow nuzzled her hand. "Sorrel's right," she said gently. "Eating Mary's food clearly makes her customers happy and Shades don't like people being happy, so it's unlikely that Shades are making them eat Mary's food." She frowned. "But it is odd that there are so many people all of a sudden."

"I think we should check if there are Shades in the café," said Bracken.

Sorrel nodded. "I'll go there now and see

what I can find out."

Some Star Animals, like Sorrel and Willow, could smell when Shades had been nearby.

"Come back soon," said Ionie. Sorrel touched her nose to Ionie's and vanished.

They waited anxiously. Maia chewed a fingernail. Had someone put Shades in the café? Was dark magic involved? Maia shivered. What if something happened to Mary and she couldn't make cakes any more?

After a little while, Sorrel reappeared. "There are no Shades," she said, relief in her indigo eyes. "In fact, there was nothing of any note at the café, apart from all the people in there." She sniffed indignantly. "One of them almost trod on my tail!"

"So, no Shades but some dark magic could still be going on there," said Ionie. "Someone could be using plant or crystal magic."

"But then we're back to the fact that nothing bad is happening there," said Lottie.

"Yet," said Sorrel darkly. "I definitely think you need to watch this café closely. Something may happen soon."

"We could all offer to help there this afternoon," said Sita.

Sorrel nodded. "Keep your eyes and ears open."

"And be careful," added Willow.

"We will," the girls promised.

The Copper Kettle was heaving with customers when they went back and Mary was very glad to accept the girls' offer of help. To their disappointment, Mystic Maureen did not reappear to claim her scarf and nothing unusual happened at all. By mid-afternoon, all the cakes had run out and Mary closed early. There were some new customers getting out of a car as the girls left.

"We've driven half an hour to get here,"

said one of the men. "We came yesterday afternoon and you were open until five then."

"I'm terribly sorry, but we've completely sold out of food today and I really need to shut so I can do some more baking,"

Mary said, looking flustered.

"I'm going to be up all night," she said to the girls as the people got back into their car, looking cross. "I like it being busy but not this busy. Thanks so much for all your help today."

When Maia opened the front door and walked in, she smelled the delicious sweet aroma of cake. "Mmm," she said, going through to the kitchen.

There was a freshly baked chocolate cake on the table. Clio was decorating it with icing and chocolate buttons. "Mum really wanted some cake at lunchtime so I thought I'd do some baking," she said.

"Yum! Can I have some?" Maia asked eagerly.

"No. It's for tea when everyone's here," said Clio.

Maia scowled. "But I want cake now!"

"Have a biscuit instead," said Clio, looking taken aback.

Maia took a biscuit and stomped upstairs. She flung herself down on her bed, feeling very grumpy. *I'm just tired,* she thought. *It's been a busy day.*

By five o'clock, everyone apart from Mr Greene was home and Clio let them have some cake. Maia took a huge mouthful and a wave of disappointment washed over her. It wasn't as good as the cake from the Copper Kettle. She put the slice down and pushed her plate away.

Mrs Greene did the same with an annoyed exclamation.

"What's the matter?" said Clio in surprise. "Don't you like it?" She had taken a break from her healthy eating to have a slice.

"No. I don't like!" said Alfie grouchily. "Want diff'rent cake!"

"But this is a special cake I've just made!" said Clio. She used a fork to pick some up from his plate. "Come on, Alfie. Yum-yum!"

"Yuck! Yuck!" he said, knocking her hand away and sending the cake and his plastic plate flying on to the floor.

"Alfie! That's naughty!" Mrs Greene snapped.

"Want diff'rent cake!" Alfie started to scream as she lifted him out of his high chair. "Want it now!" He drummed his fists and heels against her.

"You're going to your

bedroom!" Mrs Greene said sharply and she carried him upstairs still screaming. "Oh, don't be such a naughty boy!" she exclaimed.

Maia blinked. Her mum was usually really patient. She turned and saw Clio's face. She looked really upset. "It's nice cake, Clio," Maia said, forcing her own crossness down. "It's really delicious." She finished her slice, but put her plate in the dishwasher before Clio could offer her another piece. She wished her mum had bought a cake from the Copper Kettle.

Maia went up to her room. She called Bracken and he jumped on the bed beside her.

"Are you all right?" he asked.

She shrugged. "I'm in a bad mood. I don't know why – I just don't feel right."

Bracken snuggled up to her. "You've had a busy day and there's been a lot to think about."

She stroked him and felt her grumpiness start to lift. It was impossible to be in a bad mood when she had him beside her. "What do you think's going on, Bracken?"

He licked her hand. "I don't know but whatever it is we'll find out and stop it."

Maia nodded. She shut her eyes, thoughts jumping round in her head: the Shades in the dolls … Mystic Maureen … the Copper Kettle … all the people there … Lottie's feeling that they were in danger … the angry people in her dream…

What did it all mean? She had the frustrating feeling that she had all the pieces of the puzzle but she just couldn't get them to fit together, and as she was trying to work it out a hidden menace was edging closer and closer.

CHAPTER NINE

Maia was on the road opposite the Copper Kettle in her pyjamas. It was still night, although the sky was just starting to lighten in the east. A movement caught her eye. A very tall, thin man in dark clothes and a balaclava was creeping up to the bay window. She saw him raise one hand and realized he was holding a brick.

SMASH! The brick shattered the window.

Maia's feet were rooted to the spot. The café alarm started to scream out as the thief climbed into the café. A minute later, he came out, carrying two large cake boxes. He ran away down the road…

Maia woke up in bed, her heart pounding.

"Maia?" said Bracken, sitting up, too, his fur ruffled.

Maia glanced at the clock. It was six a.m. "I was dreaming about the Copper Kettle. I saw someone breaking in, only it didn't feel like a dream. It felt real!" She pushed the covers off and jumped out of bed. "I need to go and see what's happening!"

She started pulling on her clothes.

"What about your parents?" Bracken said.

"I'll leave them a note saying I've gone out for a walk," said Maia. "Oh, Bracken, I hope Mary's OK – she lives above the café."

"Be careful!" he said anxiously as she pulled open her bedroom door.

Maia ran through the peaceful streets of Westcombe. Dawn was breaking and the birds were singing. The streets were deserted but, as she turned on to the main road, she saw Mary standing outside the Copper Kettle, looking at the broken window. Maia sprinted over.

"Mary, are you all right? What happened?"

Mary looked shocked. "I was asleep when suddenly I heard the sound of breaking glass and then the alarm went off. Someone broke into the café! Thank goodness I had my grandma's journal upstairs with me so they couldn't steal that and they didn't take any of my antique teddies or dolls."

"So, what *did* they steal?" asked Maia.

"Just some cakes," said Mary. "I'd put them under the counter ready for when I opened this morning and now they've gone. The strange thing is, the intruder put them in boxes and left money on the counter."

Maia blinked. The thief had paid for them!

"Oh, this is awful," said Mary, looking close to tears. "I guess I'd better get this glass swept up and ring someone to come and repair the window." She gave Maia a puzzled look. "What are you doing out at this hour?"

"Just having an early-morning walk," said Maia. "I can help you clear up."

She and Mary set to work sweeping up the glass.

"Are you going to make some more cakes?" Maia asked hungrily, looking at the space under the counter where the stolen cakes had been displayed.

"Luckily I have some more in the back,"

said Mary.

"Can I have a slice?" Maia asked eagerly.

"For breakfast? I don't think your mum would approve," said Mary with a smile. "How about one of my breakfast muffins instead?"

She fetched Maia a muffin. "Thanks," Maia said, her heart sinking as she took the muffin. She didn't know why but she just really felt like eating cake and nothing else. "I'd better go home now. I hope you get the window sorted."

Maia walked back, munching on the muffin. It was tasty but nowhere near as nice as one of Mary's cakes.

"Where have you been?" her mum asked as she went in through the front door.

"Didn't you see my note? I went for a walk. I was passing the Copper Kettle and guess what? It was broken into last night! Someone stole Mary's cakes."

"There are some left, aren't there?" her mum said apprehensively. Maia nodded.

"Phew!" Her mum looked relieved. "I was going to buy us one for tea."

"Don't leave it too late," said Maia. "Mary sold out of everything yesterday by mid-afternoon and I have to have some more cake today!" Her mouth watered at the thought of eating Mary's chocolate cake. She wished she could have some right now!

"Who breaks into a café to steal cakes?" said Ionie when they were all sitting in her bedroom later that morning, their animals beside them.

"And leaves money for them," Lottie pointed out. "Why not just wait until the café opens?"

"It's so weird," said Sita. "Though I would really like some cake right now."

Willow nuzzled her. "I told you that you should have had some breakfast."

Sita shrugged. "I didn't feel like cereal. I just wanted cake."

"You didn't have breakfast either, did you, Maia?" said Bracken, nudging her with his nose.

"No." Maia had looked in the cupboards and fridge but, just like the day before, nothing had really appealed. Hunger pangs were now gnawing at her stomach, making her feel grouchy.

"Have you tried using your magic to see who the thief was, Maia?" Ionie asked.

Maia was too busy picturing a chocolate cake to reply.

"Earth to Maia!" said Ionie, waving a hand in front of her friend's face.

"What?" said Maia.

"Weren't you listening to me? I said why don't you use magic to see what happened at the café?" Ionie said impatiently.

Maia scowled. She didn't want to do magic. All she really wanted to do was to eat cake but she saw that everyone was looking at her expectantly.

She took out her mirror. They really should find out who had broken in and stolen the cakes. She pictured the cakes that had been taken and her tummy rumbled loudly. *Mmm. Chocolate cake...*

"Maia!" Lottie exclaimed. "What are you doing?"

Maia realized she was staring into space again. "Oh ... um ... sorry." She forced her mind to concentrate and connected to the magic current. "Show me who stole the cakes," she said to the mirror.

The magic showed her a tall, thin man dressed all in black, just as she had seen in her dream. He threw a brick through the window of the café. "Show me the thief's face," Maia said but, although the magic zoomed in, the man's face was hidden by a woolly balaclava pulled over his head.

"I can't see who the thief is," she said. "It looks a bit like Mike judging by the size and shape but it can't be. He'd never break in anywhere." She watched as the thief climbed in through the window and then reappeared, carrying two large cake boxes. Where had those cakes gone? Had the thief eaten them? Might there be some left? Maia's mouth watered and then she realized the image had vanished from the mirror.

"You know, I think I really need some

cake," she said, jumping to her feet.

"Cake?" Ionie echoed.

"Yes, right now."

"Me too," said Sita, getting up. "Shall we go to the Copper Kettle?"

Maia nodded.

"Are you both feeling OK?" said Lottie in astonishment.

"Yes, we just want cake," said Sita, an unusually determined look on her face.

"You're both cake-obsessed!" said Ionie, rolling her eyes.

Willow and Bracken shared a concerned look. "Sita, maybe you shouldn't go," Willow said.

"Yes, Maia. This is getting a bit odd…" Bracken began.

"We'll be back soon," Maia interrupted. "Come on, Sita." Sita didn't need any persuading.

Ignoring everyone else's puzzled looks,

they ran down the stairs and out of the house. "I don't know why but I can't stop thinking about cake," said Sita as they jogged along the street. "It's all I can think about."

"I know. Me too!" said Maia. They hurried up the road and turned towards the Copper Kettle.

Maia's heart sank as she saw the queue of people inside but, just as they reached the door, her mum came out, holding a large cake box. "Maia!" she said. "I got here early and I've got a cake! A big one!"

"Oh, wow!" gasped Maia. "Can we have it now?"

Her mum nodded. "Hop in the car."

"The others will wonder where we are," Maia said to Sita as they got in.

"Who cares!" said Sita, her eyes fixed on the cake box.

As soon as they got home, Mrs Greene cut up the cake and they each had a slice. Clio came in while they were eating. "More cake? Seriously? I'm beginning to worry about this family. What's so good about these cakes anyway?" She reached over to take the remaining slice.

"No!" Mrs Greene grabbed the plate and pulled it away from her. "It's mine!"

Clio blinked in shock. "OK," she said slowly. "You can have it, Mum." She backed out of the room as Mrs Greene started to greedily devour the last slice.

"Me full," said Alfie, patting his tummy.

Maia nodded and sat back in her chair with a loud, contented sigh. Her grumpiness had melted away. All she'd needed was cake! "Should we go upstairs?" she asked Sita. She was feeling a little guilty that they had rushed off, leaving Ionie and Lottie. She pulled out her phone to text them and saw that Ionie had sent a message an hour ago.

> Where are u? L and I went 2 the CK but we cdn't find u. It's really busy! We're going 2 offer 2 help. Ixx

Then there were several other messages from her.

> Maia?

> Maia? Why aren't u answering?

> Where ARE u?

"Ionie's left me loads of message," Maia said guiltily.

"Me too," said Sita, checking her phone.

"We'd better reply," said Maia, as she

started to type.

> Hi. Sorry. We met my mum and came back 2 mine 2 have some cake. Do u want to come round? Mxx

Ionie's reply came back in just a few seconds.

> We're coming now. We think we have an idea about what's going on. Stay where u are! Ixx

Maia's fingers flew over her phone.

> Really? What? Mx

> We'll talk when we see u. Ixx

Maia put her phone down. "They're both coming here. Ionie says they've had an idea about what's happening."

Sita flopped on to Maia's beanbag. "I guess that's good, only right now I feel so full I just want to sleep."

"Me too," said Maia with a yawn. "We could have a lie-down while we're waiting." She lay back on her bed with a sigh and the next moment was fast asleep.

Buzzzz! Buzzzz! Maia heard her phone vibrating and blinked her eyes open. She'd been deep in a dream where she had been at the Copper Kettle, eating an entire cake on her own. It tasted delicious! For a moment, she struggled to remember what day it was and what she was doing. She saw Sita curled up on the beanbag and remembered.

Picking up her buzzing phone, she saw Ionie was ringing her. She answered the call, feeling groggy. "Hi."

"Where are you?" said Ionie. "We've been knocking on the door but no one's answering!"

"Sorry! Sita and I fell asleep. I'll come and let you in." Maia got up and shook Sita's shoulder. "Sita, the others are here."

Sita shrugged her off. "Mmm, cake," she murmured in her sleep.

Maia went downstairs, wondering why her mum hadn't let Ionie and Lottie in, but as she passed her parents' bedroom she heard her mum and Alfie snoring. That was weird. Her mum never had naps during the day.

"Hi," she said, opening the door and letting Ionie and Lottie in. "Sorry about that. We had cake and then we all fell asleep." She saw Ionie and Lottie exchange looks. "So what's your idea?"

"Let's talk in your room," said Ionie. "We can call the animals then. I think we need them with us."

As Maia turned to go upstairs, she glanced through the open kitchen door and saw the plate that the cake had been on. There were still some crumbs and scrapings of chocolate icing on it. She felt gripped by the desire to eat them.

"Wait a sec." Going into the kitchen, she reached to scoop up the remains of the crumbs and icing with her finger.

"No!" Ionie and Lottie said together.

Ionie raced over and grabbed her arm. "Don't do that."

"What? Why?" Maia said in surprise.

"Just don't," said Ionie.

Maia started to feel anger build up inside her. "But I want to." Pulling her arm away from Ionie, she lunged for the plate. But Ionie grabbed it and lifted it out of her reach

before she could get to it.

Maia felt rage fill her. She wanted cake — she needed cake! "Give it to me!" she cried angrily.

Ionie dodged round the other side of the table. "No. You're not having it!"

"Why?" Maia cried.

"Don't you see, Maia?" Lottie exclaimed. "The cake from the Copper Kettle is making you act really weirdly. It must have some kind of magic in it."

"Dark magic," added Ionie. "Everyone who eats those cakes is becoming obsessed with them."

Shock stopped Maia in her tracks. Magic in the cakes!

"We really need to talk," Ionie said. "Let's go to your room." She put the plate down and then she and Lottie took hold of Maia's arms and marched her upstairs.

CHAPTER TEN

The four girls and their animals sat in a circle on the floor in Maia's bedroom. Maia had Bracken on her lap and, as she stroked him, she felt the longing for cake fading away slightly.

"Keep cuddling Willow," she advised Sita. "It'll help."

Sita wrapped her arms round Willow. "So it's not someone trapping Shades to cause trouble, it's someone doing something to Mary's cakes," she said. "That's why Maia and

I have been affected – we've both eaten the cakes there."

"My mum, dad and Alfie, too," said Maia.

"I thought it was peculiar that you kept wanting to eat more cake," Bracken said to Maia. "And that you were dreaming about it."

Looking back, Maia could see how odd it was that she had wanted cake quite so much.

"They are nice cakes, though," sighed Sita. "That chocolate one. Mmm…"

A picture of one of Mary's chocolate cakes oozing with icing leaped into Maia's mind and she felt hunger start to swirl up inside her, blocking everything out. She buried her face in Bracken's fur, breathing in his sweet smell until the longing faded.

"It's such a weird feeling," she explained to the others. "It's like all you can think about is cake. It fills your thoughts. You want it so much you feel as if you'd do anything to have it."

"You feel like you'd fight someone to get cake," Sita added. "Nothing else matters."

"What sort of magic is this?" Ionie asked Sorrel.

"I suspect a charm," said Sorrel. "A spell brewed with herbs could have been put into the cake mixture."

"So, the images of the Copper Kettle that I've been seeing maybe aren't to do with the Shades after all," said Maia. "The Star Magic could have been trying to warn me that someone was using magic in the cakes at the café."

"Mary?" said Lottie.

"Possibly, but the magic hasn't shown me her," said Maia, confused. "The only person I've seen is Mystic Maureen. Do you think the dolls and the magic cakes are linked? That Mystic Maureen is responsible for both things?"

Ionie looked thoughtful. "We know she goes to the Copper Kettle. Maybe she wanted to upset Mary and snuck into the kitchen and added something to the flour or sugar."

"Or maybe it's not Mystic Maureen – perhaps it's Desmond Hannigan?" Lottie put in. "We know he doesn't like Mike so he could have put the Shades in the dolls, and Maia and Sita both saw him in the café acting strangely."

Maia gasped. "Perhaps he and Mystic Maureen are in this together!"

"They could be working as a team!" exclaimed Bracken.

Juniper jumped around, chattering excitedly. "Yes! Yes!"

"Wait!" said Sita. "It doesn't make sense. Why would Mystic Maureen or Desmond Hannigan want to make people desperate to eat Mary's cakes?"

"I can see that Desmond Hannigan might want the cakes to taste horrible so no one would go to the Copper Kettle, but why would he want to make them taste so good that people can't stop eating them? You're right – it doesn't make sense," Ionie reasoned.

"The spell doesn't just make people want to eat cake, though," said Maia, thinking of her family. "It's making people really angry. Maybe that's why he was doing it."

"But it's meant business is booming for Mary and his café is losing custom," said Ionie.

"It's all so confusing!" said Lottie in

frustration. "Are the Shades and the cakes linked?"

"Maia, why don't you use magic and see if it shows you anything that can help us work this out?" suggested Willow.

Maia pulled her mirror out of her pocket and drew on the magic current. "Show me anything that can help," she told it and an image appeared.

"I can see the Copper Kettle," she told the others. "It's heaving with people. Ooh." She blinked as she took in the whole scene. "Two people are fighting over a cake and there's lots of arguing. Mary looks really worried."

The image changed.

"It's showing me something else," Maia said. "It's that picture I've seen before of Mystic Maureen in front of a mirror with lights all around it." Maia saw something she hadn't noticed before. On the dressing table, there was an old brown book. It looked just like Mary's grandma's journal…

She frowned. Why did Mystic Maureen have Mary's grandma's journal? She noticed there was some faded gold writing on the cover.

"Show me the journal in the picture," she told the magic.

"What journal?" asked Ionie, who couldn't see anything.

Maia waved for her to be quiet as the magic zoomed in on the journal so she could read the words on the cover properly: *Magic Recipes*.

"Magic!" she gasped, looking up at the others. "Mary's recipe book from her grandma has magic recipes in it!"

The animals leaped to their feet and the girls started talking all at once.

"That journal's not just a book of baking, it's a book of magic!" Sita gasped.

"No wonder she was worried that someone might try to steal it," said Maia. "Mary always says there's a bit of magic in the ice cream. I thought she was joking but she must have been telling the truth!"

"A bit of magic in the ice cream and a lot in the cakes," said Ionie. "Mary must be making magic cakes! But why would she want to make people angry?"

"And what have the cakes got to do with the dolls and the Shades?" said Lottie. "Mary is really good friends with Mike and Ana – she wouldn't want to upset them. And the magic showed Mystic Maureen with the book, not Mary. Are we looking for two people doing dark magic or one?"

Ionie got to her feet. "We need to talk

to Mary."

"Sita, you might have to use your powers," said Sorrel. "If she is doing dark magic, then you must be ready to command her to obey you."

Sita nodded confidently. "OK. I'll be ready."

For a moment, Maia remembered how nervous Sita used to be about doing magic when she had first discovered her abilities. Using magic and being Star Friends had changed them all since last autumn.

Ionie pointed to the shadows beside Maia's wardrobe. "I vote we take the quickest way to the Copper Kettle!" she said.

Bracken licked Maia's hand. "Good luck!"

Ionie was waiting in the shadows. Maia, Lottie and Sita stepped forward, held hands, then the shadows closed round them and the magic whisked them away.

CHAPTER ELEVEN

The shadows cleared and Maia saw that Ionie had transported them to the woods just across the main road from the Copper Kettle. "I didn't dare risk us appearing inside," said Ionie.

"It doesn't look like there'd be room anyway!" Maia exclaimed.

Through the windows she could see people filling every bit of space. They were elbowing each other out of the way as they tried to get to the counter to buy cakes. Raised, angry voices floated across the road to the girls.

"It doesn't look good," said Sita.

"Come on, let's see if we can help – if we can get rid of everyone, then maybe we can talk to Mary on her own," said Maia.

She led the way across the road and they pushed their way inside. People were crowded round the counter, yelling at Mary, who was close to tears.

"I want to buy cake!"

"Sell us cake!"

Their faces were red and angry. Maia spotted Mike's tall, thin figure at the front, banging his fists on the counter. A memory stirred. Had he been the man who broke in? She would never have thought it possible but right now he looked angry enough to do anything.

Maia motioned to the others and they edged their way closer to the counter.

"Go away! Please!" Mary pleaded. If she was the one doing dark magic, it didn't look as if it was making her happy.

"No!" yelled an older man. "I want cake!"
Maia realized it was her next-door neighbour,
friendly Mr Jones.

A woman picked up a salt cellar. It was
Maia's teacher, Miss Harris. "Give us cake!"
she screamed. She threw the cellar at the wall
behind Mary. It hit one of the old Victorian
dolls that were balanced on the shelves. The
doll fell to the ground.

"Be careful!" gasped Mary.

Maia ducked underneath the partition and the others followed.

"Girls, what are you doing here?" Mary turned panicked eyes on them. "You could get hurt."

"Gran!" exclaimed Sita in horror as she spotted her granny in the crowd.

But her granny didn't even seem to notice her. Her eyes were glazed over as though she was possessed. She picked up a sugar bowl and hurled it at the wall.

"CAKE!" everyone shouted, starting to throw anything they could get their hands on – plates, saucers, spoons…

"Quick, let's get out of here!" cried Ionie, ducking as a plate smashed against the wall above her head. She ran to the door that led upstairs to Mary's flat and pulled it open. "Mary! Come on!"

The customers started climbing over the

counter. Maia pushed her friends through the door and slammed it shut behind them. Luckily there was a key in the lock. She turned it quickly and was only just in time. The people on the other side started battering at the door, banging and yelling. Maia's scalp prickled as she realized it was the door she had seen in her dream.

"CAKE! CAKE! CAKE!" they shouted.

Mary rushed up the stairs to her flat and the girls followed. "Oh, what am I going to do?" she cried. "They've all gone crazy."

"Or rather they've eaten cake with a magic charm inside it…" said Ionie pointedly.

Mary's face paled. "How do you know?"

Maia spotted the journal on the coffee table. "Magic recipes," she said, picking it up. "You've been using magic, haven't you, Mary?"

Mary started to shake her head. "No … no…"

"Enough!" Sita cut in. Her voice sounded stern, completely unlike her usual soft tone, and Maia realized she was using her powers. Mary fell silent. "People are going to get hurt, Mary, if this carries on," Sita continued. "We have to stop it. We can help you but you must tell us the truth. Have you been using magic?"

Mary nodded. "I have. I didn't mean for it to end up like this. I just wanted people to want to eat my cakes." She picked up the journal. "My granny was fascinated by magic and used charms made from plants to help people with illnesses and to make her food taste good. When she died, she left me her book with all her magical notes in. I've only ever used it to add just a little magic charm to my ice cream but, when all my customers started going to the marina, I thought I'd use it to make cakes people couldn't resist."

"It certainly worked!" said Ionie.

"I didn't realize this would happen," Mary said anxiously. "I just wanted more customers. It's all got completely out of control. I can't believe the magic is so powerful that people are smashing plates, breaking in…"

Someone on the other side of the door now seemed to be using something large to try to break it down.

"What am I going to do?" Mary said fearfully.

"Don't worry," Sita said. "We're going to sort this out and, while we're doing that, you're going to go to your room and have a little nap. You will go to sleep until I wake you. Do you understand?"

Mary nodded, stood up and moved like a sleepwalker to her bedroom.

"Well done, Sita," Maia said. "Now what?"

"Now we sort this chaos out," said Sita grimly.

The girls hurried to the staircase that led down to the door into the café. The banging and hammering were getting even louder. "How are we going to get rid of everyone?" shouted Lottie above the noise.

"Let's call the animals and see if they have any ideas," said Maia.

The animals appeared and listened while the girls told them what was going on.

"You can't open that door," said Sorrel in alarm. "All those people will come charging in here and they sound full of rage. There's no knowing what they'll do."

"But we must get Sita into the café so she can command them to go home," said Maia.

"We need a distraction so Sita can get through the door and into the café," said Willow.

Juniper leaped on to the windowsill. "I know! I can get through the landing window and into the café, and Lottie can climb down after me, using her agility! I bet between us we can get everyone away from the door!"

"Good plan, Juniper!" In a flash, Lottie was by the window. She opened it and Juniper leaped out. Lottie grinned at the others. "See you in a bit!" She followed Juniper out of the window.

The others raced to the bottom of the stairs. A minute later, they heard the angry shouts turning to cries of surprise. "There's a squirrel in here!"

"What's it doing? It's leaping about everywhere!"

There was a scream. "It's on my head! Get it off me!"

"Cake!" they heard Lottie shout. "Hey, everyone, there's cake over here!"

"Cake? Where?"

"Where's the cake?"

The banging on the door stopped. Maia took her chance and pushed the door open.

Everyone was either looking at Lottie or at Juniper. As well as Mike, Miss Harris, Mr Jones and Sita's gran, she could see Elissa, Harriet and Sadie – girls from their class.

"Go!" she hissed to the animals.

They leaped into the café, making people shout and stagger, forgetting about cake in their surprise and confusion. "A fox!"

"A deer and a cat!"

"What's going on?"

"Now, Sita!" exclaimed Maia, pulling a chair over to the counter.

"QUIET!" Sita commanded, climbing up on to the counter. "No one must speak or move again until I command it." The whole room fell still. Maia tried to open her mouth and found that she couldn't speak either. The animals were also frozen to the spot. "Maia, Ionie, Lottie and the animals, you can all move and speak," Sita said hastily, realizing what she'd done. Maia felt a rush of relief as her body and voice came under her control again. Sita's magic was really powerful and scary!

Sita cleared her throat. "Everyone apart from Ionie, Lottie, Maia and the animals – you are all to go home. You do not want to eat cake any more. When you walk out of the door, you will forget about everything that has happened in here. You will go home and feel relaxed and happy, thinking what a lovely time you've had at the Copper Kettle and wanting to come back again soon."

Maia was impressed. Sita had become very good at giving magic commands.

"Now go!" Sita instructed. Suddenly everyone started moving again. The girls watched as people dazedly rubbed their heads and wandered out on to the street, their anger and desire for cake completely forgotten. Sita's granny hesitated, looking at her. "Go home, Gran," Sita said forcefully, and her granny nodded and left.

As the last person went out, Willow butted the door shut. Lottie joined her, locked the door and turned the sign that said *Open* to *Closed*. "Phew!" she exclaimed.

Ionie looked at the doorway that led upstairs. "Time to go and talk to Mary," she said.

They went upstairs to the flat. Mary's bedroom door was open and they could see she was still asleep, lying on top of the covers, breathing peacefully. As they walked in, Maia stopped in her tracks. Mary's dressing table was opposite the bed. It had a mirror surrounded by lights, exactly the same as the one that she had seen Mystic Maureen sitting at. But why would Mystic Maureen have been in Mary's bedroom unless … unless…

Her eyes caught sight of the multicoloured scarf hanging over the back of the chair and, on top of it, was a beaded necklace with a large M hanging from it.

It was as if a flashbulb had gone off in Maia's head. Suddenly she realized why the image of Mystic Maureen sitting at the mirror had always niggled at her. The reflection in the mirror had shown Mystic Maureen with her shoulder-length red hair but from the back the figure had short brown hair and had looked just like…

"Mary!" she exclaimed. "Mary is Mystic Maureen!"

Chapter Twelve

Everyone stared at Maia.

"What do you mean?" demanded Lottie.

"Have you solved the mystery, Maia?" Bracken asked, bouncing around in delight.

"I think so. Look!" Maia grabbed the necklace with the M pendant from the chair and the scarf. "Mystic Maureen was wearing this necklace and this scarf. Mary must have disguised herself as her with magic."

"Using a glamour!" Ionie exclaimed. She hit her head. "Of course! Why didn't

I think of that?"

"It all makes sense now. It's why the Copper Kettle kept appearing in my visions! I even knew that Mary collected dolls just like Mystic Maureen said she did," Maia said, glancing at the dolls on the shelf and thinking of the others downstairs. "I just didn't put it all together!"

"No wonder we haven't been able to find where Mystic Maureen lives or works," said Lottie. "She never really existed. She was Mary in disguise!"

"But why?" Sita said. "I thought she liked Mike and Ana."

"I think you need to wake her up and ask her about it," Sorrel said.

"Hide," Ionie urged the animals. "Sita can make her forget you, but if she sees you she's bound to ask questions and we want to find out what's been going on as quickly as possible."

The animals vanished.

"Do your stuff then, Sita," said Maia.

The others nodded.

"Mary," said Sita, going over to the bed. "I want you to wake up now."

Mary stirred, mumbling a little in her sleep. Rubbing her eyes, she sat up. "What's happening?" she said dazedly and then her eyes widened as she remembered. "The café! The people!"

"It's all right," said Sita soothingly. "They've all gone. There's nothing for you to worry about now. Just a bit of clearing up to do."

Mary relaxed. "Oh, thank goodness." She looked at Sita anxiously. "You won't tell anyone I put a charm in the cakes, will you?"

"No," said Sita. "But you mustn't do it any more."

Mary nodded. "I won't. I wanted business to pick up, but I shouldn't have used magic the way I did. It isn't the answer." She rubbed her forehead. "It can be so hard to control."

"Mary, have you used magic before? Did you use it to disguise yourself as Mystic Maureen? And to conjure Shades?" Sita asked.

Even though Maia knew the answer, it was still a shock when Mary nodded.

"But why?" Lottie burst out.

"I just wanted to help," Mary said unhappily.

"Help?" echoed Ionie. "But how could conjuring Shades help? They're evil."

"I didn't realize that," Mary said. "There were notes at the back of the journal about all sorts of different magic – using glamours, conjuring Shades. It didn't say Shades were evil and I just thought if I conjured Heart's

Desire Shades they would make Mike's wish to win the Best Kept Village competition come true, and if that happened the Copper Kettle would get busier. I didn't know that they would do all those awful things. I wanted to stop them, but I didn't know how. Thankfully one day they just vanished."

The girls exchanged looks. The Shades had only stopped when Ionie had sent them back to the shadows, but Mary didn't need to know that.

"So, how did you do it?" Sita asked. "How did you trap the Shades in Ana's dolls?"

"I went to their house, disguised as Mystic Maureen, and when I was there I used my phone."

"Your phone?" repeated Maia. "How?"

"My grandma had written that a Shade can be trapped if you capture its likeness. I conjured them with my grandma's magic spell and then trapped them by taking photos with my phone."

Suddenly another of the clues Maia had seen made sense – the rectangular black object was an old-fashioned phone with buttons, not a remote control!

"Then what did you do?" Sita asked.

"I went to Ana's and transferred the Shades from my phone to the dolls. I wish I'd never done it." Her eyes filled with tears. "I feel so guilty."

Maia didn't know what to do. They'd never had to deal with someone who'd been using dark magic to try to do good before.

Sita took Mary's hand. "It's all right, Mary. You're going to get up and then we're all going to go downstairs and help tidy up," she instructed. "You're going to forget that we know about magic. You're going to feel relieved that the magic cake has all gone and you're going to decide that you will never use your grandma's magic book ever again, apart from to add a little magic to the ice cream. Do you understand?"

"I understand," said Mary, her eyes on Sita's.

"Then let's go and tidy up," said Sita, helping Mary off the bed.

They went downstairs and began clearing away the broken china and cleaning the tables. They carefully swept up any remaining crumbs of cake. Maia's tummy rumbled at the sight of them. She longed to grab them and eat them, but she fought the urge. *No cake,* she told herself firmly. *The cake is bad.* Lottie saw her face and quickly put the crumbs in the bin.

They were nearly finished when there was a knock on the door.

"It's Desmond Hannigan," Maia said in surprise. They'd been wrong about him being involved, but why was he here now?

Mary went to the door and unlocked it. "I'm afraid we're closed at the moment."

"I don't want to have a cup of tea or buy

a cake," he said brusquely. "I'm here with a business proposition for you. Can I come in?"

Mary opened the door and he walked in.

"It's come to my attention that the ice cream you sell here is far superior to the ice cream that's on sale at the marina café," he said, clearing his throat. "I want to know whether you would be interested in supplying your ice cream to the Friendly Fish from now on."

"That's a brilliant idea," Maia said in delight. "You'll make lots of money, Mary, and then it won't matter if the Copper Kettle is a bit quiet."

But, to her surprise, Mary looked worried. "I don't know. I've never supplied another business before."

"It'd be great!" said Ionie. "Selling your ice cream at the marina would mean lots more people could enjoy it."

"I'd have to employ another member of staff and buy more equipment," Mary fretted. "It would be quite different."

"Maybe," said Sita. "But that doesn't mean it'd be bad. When things change, life often gets even better." She gave Maia a quick smile. "I realized that yesterday."

Mary nodded slowly. 'I suppose so. After all, it was a big change when I started the Copper Kettle and that worked out for the best."

Desmond Hannigan cleared his throat. "So, do you want to come into business with me?" he asked.

The girls looked hopefully at Mary.

"Yes," she said, smiling. "I do."

After the café was cleaned up and Mary happily settled back upstairs, working out how she could make enough ice cream for two businesses, the girls ran to the clearing.

"Bracken!"

"Sorrel!"

"Juniper!"

"Willow!"

The animals appeared, questions tumbling out of them.

"What happened?" said Bracken.

"Did you sort everything out?" asked Willow.

"What happened to the cake?" demanded Juniper.

"Did you stop that woman doing magic?" Sorrel said sharply.

"Yes, it's all sorted," said Maia happily.

"Mary never meant to hurt anyone," Ionie

said, crouching down and stroking Sorrel. "She only wanted to help Mike and her business. She didn't realize she was doing such powerful magic. It just got out of control."

"She's never going to use that magic journal again," Sita told Willow.

"And all the magic cake has been thrown away," Lottie said, cuddling Juniper.

"She's also agreed to make ice cream for the marina," said Maia. "Which means the Copper Kettle will stay open even if there aren't quite so many customers."

"That'll probably suit Mary," said Sita. "I don't think she liked being so busy!"

"Everything's worked out perfectly," Maia declared. "There's nothing to worry about any more." She glanced at Sita. "Is there?"

Sita smiled. "No. If I can stop an angry mob of bewitched people, I think I'll be able to cope with SATs. I'm not even going to worry about starting secondary school. It'll be a big change but it'll be fine. We're all going to stay best friends, carry on fighting dark magic and making people happy, and that's all that really matters."

Willow rubbed her head against her. "I've been telling you that for weeks."

Sita kissed her. "I know. I should have listened to you."

"Don't forget we've still got one more term at Westcombe to go before we leave," said Lottie. "OK, I doubt Mum will let me out of the house while we're doing SATs but after that we've got the school trip! It is kind of scary, but I bet it'll be fun."

"We've also got sports day and the Year Six play to look forward to," put in Maia.

"And the end-of-year maths challenge!" said Ionie, beaming.

"Yay!" said Lottie excitedly.

Maia and Sita shook their heads at each other and grinned.

Maia held up her hand for a high five. "Whatever happens, we all know that magic is forever!"

The others met her hand with theirs. "Forever!" they echoed and then they all spun away, laughing.

Lottie chased after Juniper while Willow cantered away with Sita in pursuit. Sorrel pressed against Ionie's legs, purring loudly.

Maia crouched down and Bracken put a paw on her knee. Happiness rushed through her as she gathered him in her arms and he licked her nose.

"Things may change this year but we're going to love each other forever, aren't we, Bracken?" she whispered. "Whatever happens, wherever I go, you'll always be with me, won't you?"

"Always," he promised, his soft fur tickling her face and his eyes shining star-bright.

About the Author

Linda Chapman is the best-selling author of over 200 books. The biggest compliment Linda can have is for a child to tell her they became a reader after reading one of her books. Linda lives in a cottage with a tower in Leicestershire with her husband, three children, three dogs and three ponies. When she's not writing, Linda likes to ride, read and visit schools and libraries to talk to people about writing.

www.lindachapmanauthor.co.uk

About the Illustrator

Lucy Fleming has been an avid doodler and bookworm since early childhood. Drawing always seemed like so much fun but she never dreamed it could be a full-time job! She lives and works in a small town in England with her partner and a little black cat. When not at her desk she likes nothing more than to be outdoors in the sunshine with a hot cup of tea.

www.lucyflemingillustrations.com